MCBUNGLE'S AFRICAN SAFARI

Brenda Parkes
illustrated by Ester Kasepuu

RIGBY
EDUCATION

Professor McBungle
Had retired with his wife
To a house in the country
To lead a quiet life.

One day the McBungles
had nothing to do
So off they went to visit the zoo.

And that very night they decided to get
A simply
STUPENDOUS
SPLENDIFEROUS pet.

In early September
Professor McBungle
Set off in his jeep
For the African jungle.

After a while
He came to the Nile.
"Ah! Here's where I'll find
A big crocodile."

McBungle climbed down from his jeep
To a place where crocodiles might sleep.

McBungle searched far.
McBungle searched near.
He searched ALL the places
Where crocodiles appear.

"Oh dear! Oh dear!
No crocodiles here!"

"An elephant is the next on our list
Surely an elephant can't be missed!"

"Ah! Elephant footprints,
I'll follow these."
So he followed the footprints
Under the trees.

McBungle searched high.
McBungle searched low.
He searched ALL the places
Where elephants go.

"Oh dear! Oh dear!
No elephants here!"

"I'll keep on searching.
I'll keep on trying.
Maybe today I'll find a lion."
McBungle searched till he found a cave.
He crept right up, feeling awfully brave.

"This looks like a lion's lair.
I'm sure I'll find a lion in there."

McBungle searched inside.
McBungle searched outside.
He searched all the places
Where a lion just MIGHT hide.

"Oh dear! Oh dear! No lions here!"

List of
Animals
Crocodile X
Elephant X
Lion X
Monkey

"I've looked and I've looked
But I seemed to have missed
All the animals on our list.
But I won't give in
And I won't go away
Perhaps I'll find a monkey today."

"Ah! Banana skins lying on the ground!
Where there're bananas,
Monkeys can be found."

McBungle searched East.
McBungle searched West.
He searched ALL the places
That monkeys like best.

"Oh dear! Oh dear!
No monkeys here!"

So late in December
Professor McBungle
Drove his jeep OUT of
The African jungle.

Puzzled and frowning
And shaking his head.
"Maybe I'll look in
Australia instead."

From places all over
The African jungle
The animals watched
The departure of McBungle.